Rainbow Iris

by Eliana Joy

Rainbow Iris

ISBN: 9798464468641

Imprint: Independently published

<u>Chapter 1</u>

In all of Teffa, no matter how high the heavens stretched or deep its gem-filled caverns ran, it was a green and emerald world. Every tint and hue whether saturated or dull was green.

The world was lacking in human and animal life but filled with flowers, grasses, and tall-standing trees. This was a world of plants and abandoned cities. Yes, a magnificent land where mansions stood forever without decay. The world left an innocent song, one of a palace trapped in a time capsule.

Trees never lost their branches, and the grass never reached its maturity, always standing three inches up without falling over. Homes were filled with glittery, magic potions and enchanted mirrors. A world of mystery and stories untold.

And in this green world was a certain young woman—who wasn't very young at all—whose name was Greenie. She was a peculiar girl—one of a very odd nature; A woman who dreamt in color. When she went on about the colors she loved so much, her eyes would light into a rainbow and dance like the reflection of a soft river's bay.

Miss Greenie was several hundred years old yet with the beauty of a young maiden hanging on her face. And, no, she wasn't a witch. Greenie was an immortal living in a world without any other creature of her intelligence to interact with. And being so, Greenie had developed a special method of communication.

She talked to herself all day long.

The girl shared her thoughts out loud every second. She narrated her days and sang like a bird.

But other than her habits, her rainbow irises, and that she was an apparent human, the woman had dark, majestic red hair that set her apart. It glowed like fire at night when she slept and lit up the sky guiding her travels. She was evidence that color existed.

"Time for berry hunting! Haha! I can't wait to see what beautiful berries I'll catch today! I mean—it isn't like the berries have ever been bad or unripe—but still what a joy to gather some berries!" Greenie chirped before throwing her legs out of her favorite castle's bed.

Greenie believed she was the only creature like herself to exist. She knew not any other. She never asked where the castles came from or the many clothes she decorated herself in daily. Dress up was one of Greenie's favorite pastime activities.

Looking into a golden mirror, she flashed her new outfit taking a spin. Holding up auburn hair, she twisted it into a waterfall ponytail letting it drape down her back. The hair in question was long enough to graze her hips when she walked, so she often placed many ribbons in it before going out.

"Time to get breakfast!" she yelled while throwing her hands to her mouth in a giggle. "The air is going to be so crisp from the morning dew. My toes are going to soak into the grass—I just can't wait to enjoy myself!"

Walking as though her toes were gripped by invisible strings, Greenie made her way to the doorway. Not before leaving—she grabbed her berry-picking basket, one of wire, and a beautiful bowtie around its handle. She displayed a pink napkin made of fine cloth over its bottom and tossed on a Victorian, white hat before leaving her castle.

Outside one might get a better view of the extent of the caliber of the castle she lived in. Its brick was pepper pink created by chiseled, red stone faded by gray paint. Its foundation was made of huge rocks showing many colors. Under the end of the castle a small, brick pathway led to a bridge with a small river and pond underneath. There, Greenie often played with her feet in the water with her dress pinned in a clip to the side.

Running through the noiseless alley where only water, wind, and footsteps marked the skies, she bounced and tossed her arms, throwing her basket up every so often and ducking below branches. "You're brave—you're bold—you're adventurous!" she had sung in a pitchy tune to herself.

"Running through the forest!
Who can pilferage their fruit?
Tist' I!

The only one—in the world!
I must be strong!
You're brave!
You're bold!
You're adventurous!"

"Hmm Hmm hmmm!" Another voice started singing. Its melody matched her rhythm, but its pitch was much deeper; Majestic.

Whose voice was this? Not once in hundreds of years of life had Greenie ever heard another voice, or a tone like that. Freight hit her heart causing it to collapse in and her stomach to turn.

"Hello?" Greenie asked, looking into the forest. Her stomach, despite its upturn, growled and desired its morning fruit.

"Well—nevertheless—I must gather my berries!" she said hesitantly at first, but her words soon turned into a scream. "Hello!" she screamed, rushing into the forest with a smile cemented on her face.

Dashing over one of her beloved rocks that was covered in a maroon tint with hanging greenery, she followed the humming. "I must be strong!" she sang hoping to encounter her duet partner. "You're brave! You're bold! You're adventurous!"

Each line was dry at first then dragged into an upbeat tune causing the trees to appear alive and her world to seem more vibrant just by words. The skies' white light pierced through the heavens of the tallest treetops.

"Hmm Hmm—" the voice continued. It was odd to Greenie as the melody never seemed to change its distance, only growing more distant as she ran closer and in as she walked away in defeat.

"This voice, oh I hope it's human!" she squealed, holding her hands together. "What if they've been here as long as I have? Do they know why I am the only human here?"

Greenie stopped and sat by the common river to rest her ankle in it which had received a scrap during her run. Gold glitter danced around her skin connecting each piece of missing skin and flowing into its place like magic. Greenie wasn't just any immoral, but an all-healing immortal who could never die even if she wanted. Death would never taste her.

Staring at the water, she peered in her mind as she imagined its blue color and a bright, yellow sky dancing off in reflection. She moved her shoulders from side to side and closed her eyes envisioning her dreams filled with color.

"Oh, how I adore colors! I know there must be some way to bring them to my world!" she sighed.

Grabbing a blade of grass she glared at it and pointed. "I know, you're at fault! Your color is green! What did you do, you lil' blade of grass!" she jested falling into a backward laugh.

"You know—I could help you bring color into this world—again," the humming voice said.

Goosebumps crawled up Greenie's back causing her arms to befall her sides. She peered in and attempted to grab the air before sinking into the water. "C-Color?!" she cried.

"Color? You can bring color into this world?" she yelled, ignoring her now-soaking, wet dress. As soon as she stood and walked out of the river, it dried completely returning the world to its timeless state.

"Well—hold on, aren't you going to ask me who I am?" the voice said.

Greenie blinked and peered around. "I would assume by now, I have lost the remnants of my sanity, but due to my lack of knowledge of that term or why it exists in my head, I can't answer who you are. Are you a voice inside of my head? Will, surely you are invisible. I ran throughout the forest looking for you for a good period. Why didn't you say something then?"

"I am sorry, I was watching you. I do not talk much, but I can help you."

In a spin, Greenie imagined the origin of the voice and ducked her head down. "It's all right. I'm just so happy to have someone to talk to. I mean other than the rocks and the trees—they're a good company as well . . ."

Seeing no face, her lips turned into a pout of puckered green that displayed light, emerald skin. "Not visible."

"I am not," they replied.

"Well—I have some questions, but tell me about the colors first!" Greenie held both of her hands together enthusiastically to her face and smiled.

"To bring color to the world—you must get a special piece of wood and fashion it into a paintbrush."

"Paintbrush, but I don't paint," she said, hunched over into her hands. This was horrid news for Greenie as she never had any luck with a brush or the artisan's charcoal. Not even a spell could make Greenie an artist.

"You don't need to be good at it . . . but I know you will do just fine. I will guide you to the brush, but the craft and the painting will be up to you. This test is going to require you to reach into the depths of your soul to make this work. Monsters will come alive and tempt you to betray me. You have to remember my voice. Don't listen to someone else's voice no matter how much you want someone to talk to. I will be here for you, Greenie." And like that—his voice vanished from Greenie's mind.

<u>Chapter 2</u>

After the voice, that Greenie named Mr. Silence, disappeared suddenly from her during the forest, she began to replay every single phrase he said to her. Several days had followed and since that time, she found herself more interested in Mr. Silence than she was in any of her chores, walks, or songs she often made.

"You sure don't talk much, do you," she muttered, dropping her third dish that morning.

She was a clumsy girl, but even so clumsier when her mind was in a daze.

If there was one talent Greenie had beyond any skill in the world it was her ability to talk. She could blab about every action and every detail of her inner-most thoughts. The girl truly wore her heart on her sleeve.

Dashing to the stables, which she knew nothing behind their design, Greenie grabbed a hay bucket which was always full throwing it among the grass. One of her games in the morning consisted of running barefoot across hay on the downhill of Teffa's green hillside.

"Maybe I should go to another castle. Maybe he doesn't live here. He said monsters would come. I should read a book on monsters—books about humans and their lives."

She held up her green, satin dress and dashed across the hay running full throttle down the hill, falling on her back, she laughed to her side. "This never grows old on me like other things."

With her arms behind her head, Greenie peered to the sky, "Last night I dreamt of splicing colors all mixed with white—like the sun, and they ran down like squished strawberries."

She didn't notice it, but when she spoke, her eyes lit up rainbow-colored and danced in a circle.

The girl had only become self-aware of her eyes when looking in the waters. She doubted their honesty because her mirror always displayed a light green color to her.

Greenie was a brave girl and independent, but she feared insanity and loneliness the most. Having dived herself into several human books on the human mind and read spell bottles, which she never used, she learned that humans alone could lose themselves and turn mad. When things didn't make sense to her or felt odd—she ignored them.

This girl was aware of her glowing red hair, but she never found a purpose for it beyond beauty. Sometimes it lit when she sang, but that was all the girl knew about her majestic, auburn hair.

Spells and potions were something Greenie stayed away from having read story after story where monsters made humans drink potions and die to take over their bodies. Monsters were the boogeymen of Teffa, always having a plot of plan that ended in a human's death or disappearance. Greed and hatred were usually a human's reasons for using potions or spells.

But despite the stories of spells and monsters being so down and dark, warnings to humans, Greenie loved fantasy stories. She read with candles every night and giggled having reread her favorite tale for the twentieth time.

She didn't just read her stories, Greenie acted them out while reading out loud. She would hold her arm out to her side or right and dance, making voices for each character.

"I wonder—I wonder if he will play with me?" Greenie questioned, thinking about her pastime activities in a world where time existed not.

"I will find that special wood and bring color to this world!" she said with a clap standing up. "Now where is Mr. Silence? Saying all those things and ignoring me for days on after!"

"I am here," Mr. Silence said, causing fright to befall Greenie. "And—I have a name, it's Emmen."

"Oh!" she squealed, almost losing her balance.

"Don't fall again," Emmen said, in an almost joyous tone.

"Emmen? Such a strange name, mine is Greenie, but you already know that. I have been thinking of the things you said to me, and I made a couple of deductions."

"Oh? Let me hear then."

Greenie pointed one of her index fingers out, "You are a silent man. I deduced you were a man or of a male nature due to the books I've read describing a man's voice.

"I also concluded you to be a stereotypical sword fighter. The kind that comes halfway in the story trying to steal the glory from the main character."

"Steal the glory—your glory?" Emmen laughed.

"Not my glory. Wait? Do you think I'm the main character? And if I am—who am I? I mean, certainly, you know who I am," Greenie said, spinning over the green grass mixed with hay. It was only a few minutes off from the hay resetting back into the carriage stall.

"I want you to walk as we talk. I'll show you the way. Go straight ahead for now. This is going to be the place that I spoke of earlier. There's a certain tree called an Edorus that you'll need to collect the wood from."

With a cheerful smile, Greenie held out both of her hands and began running forward. In a laugh, she said, "So—who am I?"

"I cannot say."

"Fine . . . Why didn't you tell me the directions sooner?'

"Because it wasn't time yet."

"Time? Time doesn't even exist. It was something the humans created."

"And why do you reason that?"

Running up and turning with a spin of her dress, Greenie snatched her hat before it flew and gazed at the many grassy hills ahead of her. "Because time means humans, animals, death, and life; Things this world doesn't have. Things I have never experienced."

"Surely time does exist, what about the sun and the moon? Or the stars and their constellations?'

"The kind that reset perfectly every month and every night changing ever slightly giving birth to the very illusion of time."

"I see. I do all things in order. Keep going but turn to the right. Follow the hillside and you'll see a riverside with trees vastly taller than the forest we met in. Gather some sticks from their branches. Then I will see you later."

"Okay! I can't believe I'm about to bring color to Teffa! Can you just smell it?"

"Smell it?"

"The change in the atmosphere! It's like the trees—they know that their bark is going to brown and the frogs—they know they'll stay the same. Everyone is in agreement about color!" She clapped her hands together and laughed as they entangled themselves together.

"You can tell it's time," Emmen said before his voice softened into a dissipating sound again.

Digging her hands into the hillside, Greenie gnawed at several pieces of dirt as warms danced in the misted fields. She pulled out grass, flinging it before her steps and laughing.

"Soon they'll be color,
Soon they'll be yellows,
Purples,
And reds,
Oh' like my hair,
Dancin' together',
We'll all shine away,
Making a rainbow,
Let's filter the air," Greenie laughed in a song.

During her many spins and kicks, Greenie managed to dodge several trips and instances which would have caused her golden sparkles of healing power to surround her.

The immortal girl never knew a normal life. She had a permanent life in every way. Glowing hair and sparkling healing abilities were all she knew.

Seeing the trees hit the horizon, Greenie sped up pulling up her dress and making a dash towards the extra-tall forest. Greenery hung down the trees like ribbons on a lady's hat. Each one draped and skirted the forest. She wasn't one for acrobatics as she was such a clutz, but the girl needed to get up high enough for a twig. Searching for a footstool and finding none, she had just the idea, to use her dress as a climbing rope.

Braving the tallest trees in all of Teffa, Greenie wore her undergarments, which were long, white stockings and a corset all of which covered any visible skin beside the chest and the knees.

"I must be strong!" Greenie chanted, lifting herself several inches. In a sigh and a huff, she managed to exert herself to a walking stance.

"Be bold!" she said. In another huff, the young girl managed to reach a limb. Though the referenced limb was thin as if it were a snake Greenie had seen in several reptile books.

She did not dare to best the limb, knowing it would concave in instead she lifted herself shortly above it and kicked with her foot. Not discerning it givining weight, she decided to place her load on the branch while holding onto her dress.

For typical, Greenie misjudged herself and toppled the branch down causing her footing to give way. In a scream, she gripped onto the dress that began to shred faster than it could autoregenerate.

"Ahhh!" she squealed, falling on her back. In a gasp of air, she laid there with her arm out towards the sun that peeked through the treetops mocking her lack of wit.

"One day—I'll make you yellow! Just you wait, your jokes grow old on me!" she yelled as her healing powers kicked in.

Her back was completely broken and that is why the girl felt almost no pain despite the seriousness of the fall. She scooted over with blood on her lip and a bruised face and grabbed the branch pulling off several pieces.

"I will spend the fullness of my life learning to paint if that's what it takes," she muttered, getting up. "Now—time to return home before sundown."

Throwing on her now stained dress and dancing in a spin, turning dry and neat, Grennie marched in the direction of her pink castle to rid herself of the memory of the fall.

This wasn't the first time Greenie had been saved from death, due to her antics, but the girl never thought of such things. She always played them off with a smile, good cheer, and a shrug.

"Oh well," Greenie whispered. "Time for eggs and bread—and oh' let's have sugar rolls!"

Sometimes, very raley, did Grennie refer to herself as we or us because the loneliness got a hold of her.

Chapter 3

Greenie gazed around at the vast display of colors. Blues and purples made love to her rainbow irises. Her green lips quivered as she ran into each splash of color.

"I love color!" she shouted, grasping at the air.

"You certainly do," Emmen's voice replied.

"But—I am dreaming," Greenie muttered. "Where are you?" she inquired.

Stepping forward and over many whites that flooded her like a river of bedsheets, the immortal girl leaped seeing a figure behind many shades. Her heart stopped noticing the form was that of man.

He was clothed in a rainbow robe of silk, and his hair draped down long and black. Walking closer, Greenie saw his eyes, a golden brown that splashed against his tan skin. His teeth were bright white, unlike Greenie's pastel green.

Emmen was a different species than Greenie altogether; He was human.

"Emmen," Greenie whispered, stepping forward and touching his cheek.

He turned his head and said, "Yes, I came to visit you. To explain the next step to you."

"Step," Greenie repeated in a daze. The man was more handsome than any storybook drawing she had ever seen. She didn't know much about love stories or love at first sight, but she knew her heart was pounding.

"Yes . . . your hair. You must pluck a piece of it and tie it around the stick. Then I will explain the rest when you wake up. Tomorrow is going to be an exciting day for you. Color will enter Teffa.

"And—Greenie—you could have found some sticks on the ground, there is a permanent supply of fallen twigs that adds to the decor of the forest. You never had to fall and get hurt like that."

"Hurt? That was nothing. I must be braver than you. Wait, you were there, and you could have told me that?!" Greenie exasperated.

"I only talk at appointed times. I'm sorry," Emmen said, looking down.

Greenie dogged her head up, slapping herself into reality having been overslept in the first place. She ran through her house skipping about. "Now—where did I leave those sticks?"

Dashing downstairs, and still in her nightgown, Greenie rushed to the pile of wood. She placed her hands on each one and held them up in exception. "Perhaps Emmen is a human ghost," she said, leaning into the stick.

"How could he visit me in my dream? I still don't know much about him. The man looked like a prince and told me monsters would come if I painted color, yet he told me how to paint color. What is his ploy? Is he truly after my main-character glory? What does that make him?"

Mumbles and mutterings followed Greenie back upstairs and to her nightstand. Her fingers were so excited that she could barely keep herself from dropping the sticks that she worked so hard to collect.

Brushing her hair over fifty times each side with a bristle brush and humming cheerful tunes,

Greenie imagined how exciting it would be to have color in the world. "My skin, will it change, maybe pinker?" she asked.

"I bet that I am human too!"

"What if I'm not human?"

"Well—even if I wasn't human, I know someone who is," Greenie giggled looking in the mirror.

"You haven't done it yet? I am surprised, truly," Emmen said, causing Greenie to fall into her vanity.

"Stop scaring me like that!" she squealed, making Emmen let out a peep of laughter.

"Sorry, I don't know how else to talk to you. Should I warn you with a hello next time?"

Standing up, Greenie patted her nightgown down and said, "A hello would do you just fine."

"Okay, hello Greenie. Why don't you try it? Just pluck a piece out and wrap it around your stick as I told you."

Rolling her eyes, Greenie reached into her vibrant, red hair and closed her eyes pulling out a piece for it to return with gold a second later.

"This isn't going to be easy," Greenie mumbled. "My hair returns to my head perfectly each time a strand gets pulled."

"That is why I am here. I will remove the regeneration from your hair allowing you to use its power, but monsters will come and try and deceive you. Never forget my voice," he said.

"I will remember your voice. I admit monsters scare a brave girl like me," she uttered.

"They are invisible to you unless you are in the border realm like I am. The realm that borders your reality from the invisible. It looks identical except the monsters are here and have claimed strongholds and dominions gaining access to droves of land for eternity unless things change. The humans sold their land and gave everything to the monsters for vanity as they were deceived, their bodies were taken and consumed after a time."

Greenie gasped. "M-Monsters destroyed every human, and now, they are going to come after me?"

"You'll be alright because I will protect you."

"Protect me, how can you do that when you are never here? And just who are you, and who am I?"

"If I tell you those answers you have to promise to trust me. I will teach you about all of it and rename you when this morning passes."

"I cannot trust you. All you do is disappear on me."

"Fine. I will tell you because I care. I will speak to you the truth, and it will be your choice whether or not to go forward with me."

"Okay."

"I am the code of this world. I control everything and all ordinances. Think of me like a book full of letters and myself as those letters. This world cannot exist without me, but they never wanted me."

"The code? A book? I l-love books . . ." Greenie said, thinking out loud then covering her blushing cheeks. "So, you were betrayed, I take it. I remember you telling me the monsters will try and get me to betray you, but I will not. You have been hurt enough. I know what it's like to have pain inside you like that."

"From your books."

"No, from my loneliness. It is a pain that is deep, and it does not go away. Silence is deafening to me, so I talk out loud. I have a routine that never changes, will not until I met you, that is. I am happy, joyful even, but deep inside I feel this pain. So many what-ifs, and color was always my hope."

"Don't worry Greenie, I vow to you that I will take away your loneliness forever if you will just have a little faith in me. I will give you the color you seek, and in the end, both of us will be happy, I promise you that."

"All right, I will put my whole trust in you because I want you to be happy." Greenie plucked the hair out noticing it didn't turn gold and wrapped it in a perfect knot around her stick.

"Why do you want me to be happy, Greenie?" he asked.

"Because—when I laid my eyes on you I fell in love. I don't know much about love, but I know love, at first sight, is real. I read it in all the romance stories., and I know it is the strongest power in the world. I know nothing can stop it once it has started."

"Love?" he said, sounding soft. "How do you know that Greenie, we only just met?"

"Because you're all I can think about. You're the only person I want to be around even if other people existed. I want to ask you a million questions and never stop asking."

"You just said you have no faith in me a few minutes ago."

"Just because you aren't brave and need to be cared for doesn't mean I'm not in love with you. I mean—sure—most of the time in love stories it is different, but I have learned to accept this quality about you."

"Haha—haha—Greenie. I am no coward. I promise you, I will protect you if you believe me or not. You can put your faith in my strength. Let me show you."

Greenie held up the brush and felt a warm touch on her hand. It drizzled like a flame and a hot oven grasping her fingers moving her wrist slightly up. "See, I have powers too," he said.

"I had no idea," Greenie gasped. She continued holding the stick with her heart pounding and looked around the room. "I can just feel you telling me to look around the room and imagine the color. I don't know how."

"Because I have given you understanding. You will not be taken off guard by anything concerning the color. I will ensure it."

With a dash of her hand and a smile on her face, Greenie hit her ceiling. Her eyes began to take the shape of rainbows until suddenly the rainbow danced out leaving her eyes white and appearing in front of her. She squealed and stood in awe holding up the rainbow.

"What is this?" she asked.

"This is Rainbow Iris, your powers and my powers combined. Now you can do more than imagine colors, you bring them into reality. The ability to pull what is invisible, your imagination, and birth it into Teffa. That is the Rainbow Iris," Emmen answered. His voice sounded fascinated even like he was amused by Greenie's new abilities. As if, he waited forever to see this come to pass.

Reaching out, with a hesitant pull back, Greenie touched the glistening rainbow. "C-Color . . ." She held it, as if to grasp it, and embraced the color as she would in any dream.

Tears fell from her eyelids lightly like soft, warm flower petals dancing on a river's stream. In a jolt of energy, Greenie dashed downstairs and started painting in her mind the entire house. "There!"

"I will call you magenta!" Greenie named the colors as she had done in her many dreams.

"Blue!"

"You—you're allowed to be green!"

"Haha," Emmen chuckled.

His warmth seemed to follow Greenie as she ran playfully through the house. "And you!"

"And you as well!"

"How about breakfast?" Emmen asked.

"W-Well I am hungry," Greenie said as she gripped her brush tightly. She walked over to the counter and stuck the brush into the ribbon of her gown.

"I'll make eggs and toasted bread. Maybe pick some berries!" she squealed as if she hadn't had the same pattern for a hundred years.

It was something about Greenie, she always had a way of making repetitive tasks seem like the most exciting event.

As she fired up her stove, Greenie grabbed two eggs that were always replenished once taken. "Do you know where eggs come from?" Emmen asked.

"Yes, what kind of fool do you take me for? They come from pantries!" Greenie answered, in an insulted tone.

"Haha! Pantries! If only it were so. Let me tell you about the humans and their chores Greenie!"

"Well—you find this funny, I don't! I have gotten eggs for hundreds of years from the pantry that is where they come from! How much older than me are you?"

"It is just a tinge of irony all, but I am sorry. I should not have laughed at you. Eggs come from hens when you go out I'll show you what a hen looks like."

"A hen? I think—I remember a book where a girl got an egg from a hen. See—I did know," Greenie grinned.

Greenie was a stubborn girl who never admitted herself to be wrong, always correcting others, but she did not know this about herself. The girl had no one to correct her but the stubbornness of her consciousness these past immortal years.

After Greenie was told about the vigorous labor humans went through just to eat, she considered their deals with monsters. The girl considered it as survival, but Emmen scolded her, insisting life was possible without magic.

"You see, this world is like something the humans would have called magic. A world without chores. A world without death. But with no birth not until you birthed the color, Greenie."

"With no birth—but things restore all the time!" Now Greenie was just shaking her head and stuffing herself with eggs at the table.

"That is just a replacement. But soon—if you wish—we can have a birth together with a new story in this world. Humans and monsters will have no correlation and humans could even have easier lives," Emmen suggested.

"We could do that?! And how, let's do that now!"

"Haha, you have to give birth to color inside Teffa first and then we will talk about it."

"So, you still did not tell me who I am," Greenie said.

A silence passed its way through the room. "I will tell you, but it won't be easy for you to hear."

"Why is that? Because I am not human like you? I don't care! Just be honest to me," Greenie replied, pleading with sincerity.

"All right, you are this world's failsafe. When this world ended. You and I were never supposed to be conscious, but due to a fluke in the system, we were made aware.

"Right before this world was to be destroyed by monsters, you gained your life and stopped the world in this state. Your existence has broken time."

Green arms began to shake, and Greenie grabbed her gut. "I-It does hurt. Did I break time? Time has seasons, crops, and birth. How can I fix it?"

"Don't be alarmed. The color's secret holds a switch to change things. I know you'll love it when it is over with."

"So this birth we can create together . . . I want to decide the color of every single thing," Greenie said joyfully, changing the subject as she did every time things became dark, cracking a joke.

"Okay, done deal as long as I can write its code."

"Psh—I wouldn't know the first thing about code."

"Haha. Yes, you've never dealt with monsters before."

"Let's go outside and show me where the hens came from," Greenie replied. She stood and yawned before spinning as she smiled in the warmth of Emmen's presence.

"I can see how excited you are, but still—I thought you wanted to know more about yourself and me."

"That can wait, I told you I want to ask you all things, didn't I? Show me the hens already!"

She ran outside grabbing a pink hat and tying its knot under her chin. Her day dress was yellow skirted with white ruffles. The top of it hung in a faded blue-grey.

Outside, fresh air kissed her face, taking Emmen's warmth from her temporarily. She looked to the right to a stable of bricks and clay. There stood stacks of yellow, tan hay.

"Here—look," Emmen whispered.

Inside Greenie's mind, she saw a vision of colored hens and heard them gawking. They moved their heads as they walked. Each one walked up a ramp and into boxes.

She placed her hands out with a confused expression. Her brows turned, and her lips caved in.

"I don't—want it like that!" she pouted.

"What? You're upset?" Emmen questioned.

Shaking her head, Greenie responded, "No, it is just—the colors." Holding her hands into the air and pointing to the clouds she started saying, "I want pink skies, blue grass, and gold, glittering clouds with a yellow sun!"

"Haha—haha! Paint it however you want, Greenie; You're in charge of the color!"

"Great!" Greenie yelled, laughing as she began to hold up her brush. The Rainbow Iris presented itself like a chariot and horse. "Splash into the heavens!" she shouted.

The Rainbow Iris, like a waved tsunami, poured out its color into the sky, slapping it pink as if a permanent sunrise. The golden clouds ran with silver glitter like rain even the grass transformed its natural color into a blue.

The heavens obeyed the immortal girl and code man as they continued to walk miles that day discussing all the things humans did. It was after much discussion that Greenie decided, by chance, to be a human in the new birth they both had planned.

Returning to her castle for the night, Emmen stayed with her until she was about to fall asleep. "I will name you Faith," he stated.

"Why Faith? It is a beautiful name . . ." Green questioned in an utterance.

"Because you had the faith to bring color into a green and emerald world. Now, you have the faith to rebirth the world with me when this is all over with," Emmen said, sounding pleased.

"What is faith to you, Emmen?" Greenie asked, turning in her bed. His warmth sat at the side of the bed.

"Faith means you can believe in the invisible thing until you see it manifested even if it takes a long time. You believed in color for hundreds of years, I saw you squint and attempt to bring it to pass thousands of items."

"And yet—I was so lonely, and you said nothing," Greenie threw her covers over her head and cuddled inside them.

"I will tell you why at a later time. I enjoyed watching you just like how you enjoy talking to me."

"Like how I love you?" Greenie sat up suddenly and peered at the room with a pout.

"Simular. I watched you sing your songs contently, dance on the hilltops, or jump into river beds. I thought to myself, how can this failsafe be so pleasant? She is the only thing withstanding this world from consumption."

Goosebumps crawled up her back. "I know I am a failsafe, and I know I stopped everything from ending. But all those times, I knew nothing."

"I see, sometimes ignorance is better, you think?"

"Sometimes . . ."

"I want to ask you something, Greenie. When this is over, and we make our story together, our birth, why don't we get married together?" Emmen's voice was soft and endearing.

Greenie turned and leaped out of bed. "M-Marriage?!" she shouted. "Like the humans do?"

"Yes, one with a white dress and flowers. Like we talked about earlier."

"Yes, yes, I know. I've read so many fairy tales like this! This is how they are supposed to end!

The handsome prince marries the princess and rescues her!"

"Prince and princess. More like code and failsafe of a forgotten world."

"Why do you have to be so down in the dumps all the time?!"Greenie held her hands out. "Hold mine," she said.

Feeling warmth surrounding her hands, Greenie's cheek turned up. "I will marry you, no matter what, I will be your bride," she stated.

"All right—so when the night ends, I want you not to listen to any other voices. I am going to go and prepare a home for us. When I get back, I will show you have to release all the color back into Teffa, and together, we will have the birth of a new creation. One where no monsters exist, and one where chores aren't so gruesome for the humans. A world like this is something you're familiar with."

"O-Okay, Emmen, but don't leave me alone for long. You made me have faith in you that you would rescue me," Greenie said.

"I will never abandon you, Faith," Emmen said. When he spoke, Greenie could feel his entire body surround her, and he placed his arms around her sides, embracing her.

Greenie leaned in, and tears fell like raindrops out of her eyelids into the wooden floor. "I am finally not alone."

Chapter 4

"Wake up, Greenie, everything is ready. I got it all done in one night."

"Emmen, but you said you wouldn't be here for some time . . ."

Emmen laughed and touched Greenie's head softly. His touch felt odd today. Somewhat cold and filled with sparks of electricity, but still it soothed her.

"Couldn't stay gone too long. I need you to do something for me today, Greenie," Emmen said.

Rubbing her eyes and sitting up, Greenie said, "What's that? I'd do anything for you, Emmen."

"I need you to go past the forest where you got the stick and into an old minor's cave. I'll explain the rest along the way."

"Okay just let me get dressed first," Greenie said gazing out of bed. She threw off her silk sheets with a padded, purple quilt.

Looking into her dresser, she pondered the possibilities. Many dresses presented themselves. Some had several long laces that draped in and out woven into thin threading others were satin. The many possibilities always got her stuck every morning.

This morning, she decided on the simplest of gowns. A simple day dress. Something a peasant would wear yet beautified due to the object coming from a castle. It was frilled in the bosom a light green and hung under a dark green.

It stuck to her skin delicately as she walked. She threw on a pair of boots under, figuring she was about to walk a couple of miles.

"You ready," Emmen called, appearing far away. It seemed in the realm he was from, he gave her distance to get dressed.

"Yes," Greenie walked about from behind the room divider and spun. "Like."

"Took you long enough. It's nice," Emmen said.

Greenie's heart dropped. Had she spent that much time picking out her outfit?

Emmen appeared to be in a rush. Every word he said sounded forced.

"Let's skip breakfast," Greenie said.

"Good, it isn't like I need to eat anyway," Emmen said.

Remaining quiet, Greenie walked downstairs and opened her castle doors. The sight stopped her outside. The grass was a vibrant blue soft like the river. Its petals dripped in a clear due like the white sun.

Greenie glared at the sun. "Enjoy your color while it lasts, I will make you yellow!"

The sky appeared neon pink while all the plants had a tinge of punk resting on them like a reversed shadow. "Beautiful," she cried.

Running in a bolt she began spinning and picked up the blue grass in her hands spinning it in a throw before falling into the grass laughing.

"Greenie, we don't have time for that," Emmen said. "We've got to get to the cavern now!"

"Why are you so insistent?" she asked.

"Because if you don't do this now, you'll be stuck in this period forever alone. The world won't have color anymore either. It's called a glitch," he said. His voice sounded gravely upset though it was but a whisper in her ears.

She shook her head and moved her arms, and together, the two left towards the cavern.

***

"You sure this is the place, Emmen?"

"Yes," he muttered. "Now go inside and I want you to cut your hair. When you cut it, certain powers will be released. You'll then place it in a pentagram on the floor."

Greenie's eyes lifted. She noticed that her hands had begun to shake. This was causing her nerves to bump.

The cave was pale like a large boulder and covered in grass. Greenery hung down like a woman's braided hair and covered the entrance. She touched her hands to the place and pulled back the vines, having never been inside this place before.

Its insides appeared broken or damaged unlike the rest of the world which remained in perfect shape. She saw the minor's tools laying about and a broken railroad. Dust filled the air causing her to cough.

"Let's go deeper. Take that knife to cut your hair with," Emmen said.

She nodded her head and picked up the knife holding it in her hands. Following deeper into the mine, a weird noise tickled Greenie's ears. It was soft like the wind but getting closer, she realized it was a mine crate stuck on a broken wheel clunking about to and fro. It was as if it was on a sea making a melody with the waves.

"Right there," Emmen said, ushering to the mine crate. "Cut your hair and place the pentagram around the bucket."

Placing the blade to her long hair she hesitated for a moment but bit her lip cutting it off. A few strands fell out of her hands before her toes.

"Get every single one!" Emmen yelled. When he raised his voice she shook back almost stumbling over herself.

"Sorry," she said. On her knees, Greenie pinched each strand and began to make a circle. She knew what a pentagram was due to her many book studies.

Once each strand was placed, Emmen said, "Perfect. Now sit in the bucket. I'm going to do something next, but everything will be okay in the end."

Greenie lifted her skirt and sat in the mining bucket and held onto her knees shaking.

Something about Emmen wasn't right today. Was this who he was?

The hair on the ground began to glow, and its red color shot into the air surrounding her in a pentagram. Greenie began screaming. "Ahhh!" she screeched. "Something isn't right!"

Laughter filled the halls, and a cold feeling fell all over Greenie's body. Her body felt like ice picked twisted together. In her eyes monsters began to flash tall and scrawny. Ones with multiple eyes and long arms. They were all colored and each one surrounded her getting closer to her body with every scream.

Greenie clenched the bucket and dug her fingertips begging for relief, but none came. The world began to flash black in white as visions to Greenie.

"C-Color . . ." she whimpered.

The Rainbow Iris came out and stood in front of her for a second causing a barrier for the pain, but it too fell under. She had brought her special paintbrush inside her pocket but was too weak to reach for its components.

Each breath felt heavy and soundless to her as her stamina dwindled.

Her fingers fell to her chest grabbing onto her heart. "My heart!" she yelled. "It hurts!"

The pain continued climbing her body. Each knot of energy brought Greenie to tears. Droll left her mouth, and she peeled to her side puking.

"Emmen! Emmen!" she cried. But there was no response.

She stood on a skating leg and heard. "Where do you think you're going, sacrifice?"

The words struck her in the heart. Sacrifice. Finally, everything made sense to her. Emmen. Just who Emmen was. Emmen was a monster who had fooled her into sacrificing herself to give the land to the monsters.

"Oh, Emmen! Emmen, You're a monster!" she shouted.

Standing on both legs she attempted to leave the bucket but fell back over until a bright light surrounded her. It was warm, not cold. All the pain from before began to leave her.

"I'm no monster, Faith," Emmen whispered.

Greenie couldn't believe it, here was Emmen manifested in front of her holding her weight. His body was translucent but like the dream, he appeared the same. He wore a rainbow robe, and his hair was long and dark.

He had called her Faith. Not once had this other voice called her by that name.

Her head fell into his chest, and she began to weep. "Emmen—Emmen I thought that man was you, but he was a monster. I'm so sorry—I betrayed you!"

"I know you did, it's okay I've already forgiven you," Emmen replied.

All around a yellow bright light shunned, and Greenie heard in the dark, "You can't do this to us!"

"I can," Emmen said. "I will have justice." With that, he held out his hand and pure white streamed like a river destroying each monster that had presented itself.

Greenie's arms held onto Emmen's shoulders with all her might. She wasn't about to let go.

"I believe in you," she whispered with her last bit of strength before passing out.

Chapter 5

Two months later, Greenie spun inside her new castle looking at herself in the mirror. Her hair still glowered a beautiful red, and its length had turned to a medium that bounced on her shoulders as playful as she was.

She remembered back to the time when Emmen saved her from the monsters and how he had told her everything after. Her eyes drifted to the lilies she had woken up to, and to Emmen's soft, brown eyes.

He told her that he was God of this world, not a mistake, like he claimed before, and the reason there were no humans anymore was because he had lost all his faith in them. He knew they would always listen to monsters and betray him. He gave up on the world. But when she, being just a failsafe, became aware, he couldn't destroy her life; It was an innocent life.

Greenie pacified his anger. She played every day and read with a content smile. He couldn't bring himself to wipe her even though she was in the image of a human which he hated. There was something about watching her smile and her peaceful existence that caused him to miss humans.

He began to fall in love with her each day. And when they met, she fell for him as well.

After saving her, he took her back to a castle created just for the two of them. She had a room made of many pastels and pinks. He decorated the palace nicer than anything she had ever witnessed. The ceilings looked like pillows and ribbons hung down like curtains on each tile. The wallpaper was a mustard gold covering the head and toe of the palace, and its outside was a bright silver-gray.

It looked like a castle from a fairy tale. Just like one from the books she loved to read. The sky kissed its rocks with a new color; Yellow. Teffa was now filled with vibrant color and an aging life. Animals of all sorts roamed and humans stalked the streets.

They were not alone anymore. Neither Emmen nor Greenie knew the peace of utter silence anymore. Together in their castle is where they would go to get away from all their worshippers.

They were the most beloved couple in Teffa having created new humans giving them lives.

Each creation they called a birth or one of their many babies together.

Turning around, Greenie smiled as Emmen walked in the door. He wore a silk rainbow nightgown that was open slightly in the front. He retained his translucent and manifested form after the border realm was mixed with the natural.

"Let's make a different birth today," he said.

Greenie blushed and ran to the bed sitting on the sheets. She folded her legs together and held out one of her hands holding her paintbrush in one. A grin plastered on her face cheek to cheek.

Emmen smiled back and sat halfway on the bed and held out one of his hands. In the middle of them appeared a rainbow with numbers floating between.

"So—the sky should be orange!" Greenie said.

"What about humans who stay age seven?" Emmen replied.

"That works, and let's make them all go to a school where God teaches them."

"Haha—so now I'm a teacher."

"I want the kids to be colorful. Each one is going to be translucent like you but they glow!"

Both sat there shaking their heads at each other and muttering the night away as they did every night. In just two months they had birthed over a hundred different worlds to rule over together.

God loved humans again and Greenie was never alone; Together they were married and lived happily ever after.

That is the story of the Rainbow Iris. A girl lost in a timeless world who meets and falls in love with her creator. Together, they create an endless amount of worlds falling more in love with each other day by day.

Made in the USA
Columbia, SC
15 November 2022

71312741R00030